To DAVID *and* MICHAEL

THE RING

MUSIC BY

ADAPTED AND ILLUSTRATED BY

THE RING

Richard Wagner

John Updike and Warren Chappell

80119

New York: Alfred·A·Knopf

L.C. Catalog card number: 64-20169

THIS IS A BORZOI BOOK, PUBLISHED BY ALFRED A. KNOPF, INC.

Text Copyright © 1964 by John Updike.

Illustrations Copyright © 1964 by Warren Chappell.
Grateful acknowledgement is made to Sam Morgenstern
who adapted the music used in this book.

The Rhine

Rhinemaidens' Song

THIS is a story of greed and love, of giants, dwarfs, and gods. It happened long ago, in Germany, the land of the mighty river Rhine. Even to this day the river glitters as if with gold— but people say it is just the sun striking the water.

In those days the gold was real: the Rhinegold, a little solid lump no bigger than a cat's head. It was guarded by three mermaids whose names were Vellgunda, Voglinda, and Flosshilda. They lived in the green water of the Rhine and spent all their time swimming and singing. Like most mermaids, they were very beautiful, and a little silly.

One day there came walking along the riverbank a dwarf called Alberic. He was the king of the small, shy people who lived in the caves and crevices of the earth. The mermaids did not know this; all they could see was that he was ugly, his face dark as coal, his body twisted like an old root. For his part, he was dazzled by their beauty. He called to them, "You are beautiful! I love you!"

They called back, "We love you!" But when he went

under the water and tried to kiss them, they swam away, their silver scales flashing, their voices bubbling and laughing. "You are ugly!" they called. "Ugly, dark, and twisted!"

Cruelly they teased him. But a growing golden glow in the green water above him caught Alberic's eyes. "What is that?" he asked, amazed. Awe filled his heart. A nugget of gold was glowing on top of a rock beneath the waves.

"Fool!" the mermaids cried. "Haven't you heard of the Rhinegold, the wonderful gold of the Rhine?"

"What is wonderful about it?"

Vellgunda told him, "The gold is magic. Whoever can make a ring of the gold will rule the world!"

Flosshilda added, "That is why our father the Rhine told us to guard the gold well."

And Voglinda said, "But it is easy, for only he who renounces love can make the Ring. And who would renounce the joy of loving and being loved? Love turns the world; it leads the forest to bloom and the birds to sing. The stars in

The Gold

Renunciation of Love

the shining sky are moved by love, and the lowliest worm obeys love's sweet power."

But Alberic, maddened by their scorn, cried, "I renounce it! If I am too ugly to be loved, then I curse love, and give up all hope of it forever!" When he said this, he became terribly strong; he tore the Rhinegold from its rock and carried it away to his cave. There he forged the magic Ring, with which he could rule the world. He enslaved his fellow dwarfs, and made them heap up gold for him. Loving no living thing, he needed power and wealth, and indeed he would have ruled the world, had it not been for Wotan.

Wotan was a god, the king of the gods, and a sad god; there is "woe" even in the sound of his name. He had lost one eye in battle, and always carried a tall gray spear he had carved from the limb of a giant ash tree that grew in the center of the forest. This spear was the token of his divinity.

Gods are not always perfect. Once Wotan had done a foolish and greedy thing. He had hired two giants, Fasolt and

The Ring

Slow and solemn

Valhalla

Majestic

Alberic's Curse on the Ring

Fafner, to build him a mighty castle called Valhalla. When the time came for them to be paid, he had nothing to give them. Indeed, the castle was so splendid, so elegant and carefully built, that there was nothing in the world wonderful enough to give in payment except Alberic's golden Ring. So Wotan, acting like a bully, stole the Ring from the dwarf and gave it to the giants. But the dwarf placed a curse on the Ring. Until it was returned to the river Rhine, there would be misery in the world. Wotan's foolishness had led to wickedness, and wickedness had led to misery. Sadly Wotan left Valhalla and wandered the world, searching for a way to put things right. Disguised as a man, he wore a blue cloak and a hat whose brim drooped to hide his empty eye.

ONE dewy morning, in a lonely wood, Wotan heard the sound of metal being beaten on an anvil. Venturing forward, he came to a grotto where an old dwarf was trying to beat together the pieces of a broken sword. The dwarf's name was Mime.

Wotan, the "Wanderer"

Mime, the Dwarf

Mime was very timid, and the stranger appearing from nowhere frightened him. He said, "Go away."

"But I am weary. I am called the Wanderer."

"Then wander away," Mime said, and hit the sword with his hammer once more. The pieces fell apart again.

The Wanderer calmly came in and sat himself on a stool. "You should be more hospitable," he said. "Let us have a battle of wits. Ask me three questions. If I can answer them, I will stay. If I cannot, you may cut off my head."

"Very well," Mime agreed, for he thought himself very clever. "What is the race that lives beneath the earth?"

Wotan answered easily. "The black elves, called Nibelungs. Their king, Alberic, with a magic Ring, forced them to mine from the glittering earth a wonderful hoard of treasure, which later was stolen from him. Now he broods darkly on how to recover the Ring and the treasure."

Mime was surprised. "True," he admitted. He himself was a Nibelung, and the brother of Alberic. "And what is the race that lives on the face of the earth?"

"The race of giants," Wotan replied. "Fasolt and Fafner were their kings. But when the Nibelungs' gold was given to them by Wotan, Fafner killed Fasolt rather than share it. Now Fafner has turned himself into a dragon, and guards the gold in a cave called Hate. He is too stupid to know how to use the Ring."

"Truly, Wanderer," Mime said, "you are wise. But tell me, what is the race that lives in the clouds above the earth?"

The Wanderer stood up and grandly brandished his gray spear of ash wood. "The gods," he said, "the gods are that race! Their home is Valhalla, and Wotan is their king. He rules by the strength of his spear!" With that, he struck the ground with his spear, and the sky thundered. Proudly Wotan lifted his head, and Mime stared terrified into the empty socket of the eye that the hat brim had hidden.

He saw that his guest was the god. Trembling, Mime said, "You are right, right a third time. Your wits have kept

The Nibelungs

The Giants

your head, now go away, go away and leave me to my work." He tried to pick up his tools.

Wotan smiled and sat down in the chair again. "You are rude," he said. "Now it is your turn to answer three questions. First, what is the race that Wotan loves most dearly?"

Mime breathed more easily, for he knew the answer. "The race of heroes," he said. "He cannot recover the Ring from Fafner without breaking his pact, so he hopes that an earthly hero will do it for him. By an earthly woman, Wotan became the father of mighty Siegmund and fair Sieglinda. Their life was unhappy, but before they died, they had a son, Siegfried, who has been raised in the deep forest by a kind and clever dwarf."

The Wanderer pleasantly nodded and asked, "Second, what is the sword that Siegfried must have if he is to kill the dragon?"

Mime knew that answer, too. "Needful," he said, "Needful is the name of the sword. Siegfried will kill the dragon and

The Race of Heroes

win the gold for the kind and clever dwarf!" And Mime danced with glee, for of course he was that very dwarf.

But Wotan frowned and asked the third question. "Who shall put the pieces together?"

And Mime wailed miserably, "I do not know, I do not know! The steel is too hard for my hammer, the pieces fall apart! And if I cannot put them together, who can?"

Wotan gave the answer. "He who has never felt fear will weld the sword Needful together again." He wrapped his blue cloak about himself and left the house of the dwarf, for he had heard Siegfried approaching.

SIEGFRIED had grown from baby to boy to man in the woods; his only friends were the bears, and the birds, and the clouds, and the trees. He wore a fur pelt, carried a hunting horn hung around his neck, and had hair the color of dark gold. Mime, puzzling over what Wotan had told him, asked this wild youth, "Have you ever felt fear?"

Siegfried was curious. "No. What is fear?"

The dwarf, who felt fear all the time, tried to explain it. "When darkness creeps into the woods, and strange whispering fills the trees, and the wide-eyed owl hoots, and the twig snaps, and a low growling gathers and grows around you— then does not your throbbing heart burst and flood your body with fear, so that your toes and fingers grow numb and your legs turn watery under you?" Mime was shaking all over. He had frightened himself.

Siegfried laughed, so that all the little pots and dishes on the dwarf's shelves hopped. "I have never felt this," he said. "It sounds wonderful, to feel fear. How can you teach me?"

Siegfried

Song to "Needful"

Mime spoke with cunning. "I know of a dragon called Fafner, who lives in a cave called Hate. He can teach you fear, if any creature can."

Siegfried bounded eagerly to the anvil. "Then I must go to him! Where is the sword?" Siegmund's sword was still in pieces, because Mime's poor magic could not put it together. But Siegfried, who knew no fear, took the pieces and filed them into shreds, melted the shreds in a white-hot fire, and poured the glittering molten metal into a new mold. When the blade had hardened, Siegfried lifted it high and with one swift stroke cut the anvil in two! Thus the sword Needful was reborn. The young hero strode through the forest to find the dragon, the old dwarf trotting by his side.

THE CAVE called Hate was at the edge of the wood, in a steep and tangled place where the sun never dared shine. Inside the cave, the dragon Fafner, once the king of the giants, slept on his heap of gold treasure, growling in his dreams. By

Fafner, the Dragon

Gloomy

the mouth of the cave, Alberic brooded and waited for the day when he might once more possess the magic Ring. He looked up from his dark thoughts. A bluish light was coming through the woods. It was the Wanderer in his cloak the color of the evening sky.

"Go away, you thief!" Alberic cried.

Wotan wearily sighed; he felt a heavy truth in the charge of thievery. His greed to have Valhalla built had led him to lie, and to steal. He was weary of the glory of being a god. He yearned to rest; death was in his bones.

"When I regain the Ring you stole from me," Alberic said, his face black with hatred, "I will not be as stupid as Fafner. I will use the Ring's power to storm Valhalla. The gods will fall, and the world will be mine!"

The Wanderer shrugged. "I no longer care. I came to watch, not to plot. A hero is near who will slay the dragon. Perhaps if you warn the monster in time, he will give you the Ring as a reward."

The dwarf jumped up and turned to the mouth of the cave and shouted, "Fafner, awake! A hero is coming to slay you! Awake, give me the Ring, and live!"

The dragon's voice answered from within the cave like the growl of a great belly. "I have, and I hold," he rumbled sluggishly. "Let me sleep."

Alberic cursed. The Wanderer laughed. In the forest a hunting horn sounded the proud golden note of Siegfried.

Siegfried's Horn Call

WHEN Siegfried stepped into the glade before the cave, sunlight broke through the shadows. His shoulders gleamed; the sword Needful flashed in his hand. Alberic and the Wanderer watched unseen. Mime, his white hair standing on end, described the dragon to Siegfried: "His jaws can open as wide as a man is tall. Poison pours from his mouth; if one drop spatters you, your flesh and bones will wilt. His tail can crush rocks and his eyes can freeze water."

Siegfried listened, unafraid. "Does the brute have a heart?"

Forest Sounds

Mime said, "Yes, in the place where men have theirs."

Siegfried lifted Needful. "Then my sword will find it." And he lay down to wait beside a stream where the dragon must come to drink. Mime hid himself. As Siegfried lay alone on the soft grass, a strange mood entered his heart. The wind in the trees caressed his ears, and he touched a tiny five-petaled flower that was growing in the moss beneath his hand. A bird began to carol. It sang and sang, and seemed to be telling the young hero something he should know. Siegfried made a whistle of a reed and tried to answer the bird. Still he could not understand. He threw away the whistle and took up his hunting horn and blew a loud blast. The dragon came out of his cave. "Ah, I see my song has attracted a beauty!" Siegfried exclaimed. Danger made him gay.

Fafner did not like jokes. "I am thirsty," he rumbled, "and now I can eat as well." He opened his gigantic jaws wide.

"What lovely teeth you have!" Siegfried said. "Come, teach me fear."

Forest Bird's Song 1

The dragon spit fire and poison from his nostrils. Siegfried leaped to one side. The dragon slashed with his heavy green tail; Siegfried quickly dodged. The dragon roared and reared up so that his breast was exposed, and Siegfried plunged his sword Needful up to the hilt in Fafner's heart. Slowly, as a mountain crumbles, the dragon died. Siegfried pulled his sword from the vast still heart, and some blood sprinkled his hand. It was still hot. Siegfried put his fingers to his mouth to suck away the burning blood, and suddenly he could understand what the bird was singing. It sang:

> *"Hero brave,*
> *Brash, and bold,*
> *Now you own*
> *The hoard of gold;*
> *Enter in*
> *The cave and bring,*
> *For yourself,*
> *The magic Ring!"*

"Thank you, feathered friend, I will take your advice!" Siegfried went into the cave called Hate and came out wearing the Ring on his finger. Now the bird sang:

"Far away
And very high,
There sleeps a maid
Surrounded by
A ring of flame;
If you would be
Brunhilda's husband,
Follow me!"

"Brunhilda?" The name tasted sweet on Siegfried's tongue, strange yet familiar, distant yet near. The ferns on the forest floor trembled; the clouds seemed to rush through the sky like white horses with manes of purple and blue. Siegfried was possessed by a need to rescue Brunhilda. "Lead, little bird —I will follow!"

Forest Bird's Song 2

Brunhilda

Mime and Alberic, those stunted brothers, emerged from hiding and tried to take the priceless Ring from Siegfried's fingers, but he walked past them as if they were no bigger than toadstools. So small do greedy people seem to a man filled with the music of love.

WOTAN the wandering god, foreseeing all, had gone ahead to the mountain where Brunhilda slept surrounded by flame. There he met Siegfried, being led by the forest bird. When the bird saw Wotan, it flew away in fear. But Siegfried knew no fear. "What are you doing here, old man?" he asked boldly. "Get out of my way."

Wotan looked sadly into the face of the hero. This was his grandson. Yet the proud boy did not know him. "You owe more respect to your elders," Wotan said.

"How odd you look!" Siegfried said. "Why do you wear such a ridiculous hat?"

"I wear it against the wind," Wotan said.

Siegfried came closer. "You have only one eye! Get out of my way, or you will lose the other."

Wotan sighed and said, "You know nothing, my son. My other eye is in your face, looking at me."

Siegfried laughed at such nonsense.

Wotan said gently, "Child, do not defy me. I am a god and the father of Siegmund, your father. It is I who have set the ring of flame around the beautiful Brunhilda, who sleeps. She was my warrior maiden and disobeyed me by seeking to protect the life of your father, though his time had come. Turn back, do not awaken her. The Ring that is on your finger belongs to the mermaids of the river Rhine. Give it back to

Magic Fire

Crisp

them. Only then will the world know peace."

Siegfried did not understand, and scoffed: "Peace is for weary old men. I am on my way to find Brunhilda, and not Wotan himself will stop me!" He walked forward. The Wanderer lifted his spear, the token of his authority. With one stroke of Needful, Siegfried cut the ash-wood spear in two.

Wotan picked up the pieces silently. His wandering was done. The power of a god was taken from him; in his heart it seemed that a great burden had been lifted. He said to the hero, "Go on, I cannot stop you." Mist swallowed the figure of the Wanderer.

SIEGFRIED climbed to the mountaintop. Here a great wall of fire seemed to bar his way. Unafraid, he walked through and not a hair on his head was burned. On a rock lay sleeping a figure in armor. Siegfried loosened the helmet and lifted it from the head of the sleeper; long golden hair like a bright sea-wave fell across the rock. Siegfried was startled; trembling,

Wall of Fire

Love

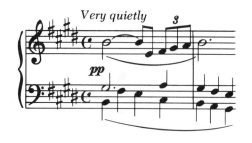

Love's Fullfilment

he delicately cut the laces of the breastplate of armor. The sleeper lay lightly clad in a woman's soft dress. She stirred; her eyelids lifted. Faced with her awakened beauty, Siegfried at last felt fear. "You have wounded me," he whispered. "I came through the fire without a shield, and your gaze has pierced my breast."

"And you have wounded me," Brunhilda answered. "You have cut away my armor, and I am but a weak woman, whose only wisdom is love, and whose only hope is to be your wife."

"Be my wife," Siegfried said, and upon her finger he slipped the Ring.

VALHALLA was doomed. Just as Wotan's spear was broken by Siegfried's sword, so the power of the gods gave way to human love. And it was Wotan himself who had willed all this. He met his own death gladly, as a traveler crosses a threshold at the end of a long journey. He ordered the great

Siegfried's Funeral March

ash tree in the middle of the forest cut down, and its wood was piled around the walls of Valhalla, and set to burning. For as Siegmund's sword needed to be melted down to be recast, so the world had to be destroyed to be born anew.

Siegfried and Brunhilda knew joy in one another, but did not live happily forever after. No human beings do. In time they died, and in dying returned the Ring to the mermaids of the Rhine, where to this day the gold may be seen glittering —though people say it is just the sun mixing with the water.

DAS ENDE

RICHARD WAGNER

[1818–1883]

THE great German composer was a poet as well. His crowning achieve-
ment, *Der Ring des Nibelungen*, was printed as a long dramatic poem,
without music, in 1853. More than twenty years passed before the music
was completed and the Ring cycle of four connected operas (*Rheingold,
Die Walküre, Siegfried*, and *Götterdämmerung*) was sung and performed
on the stage, in 1876. The performance was a national event; and the
specially constructed theater in the Bavarian town of Bayreuth has been
the scene of Wagner festivals ever since. Wagner took his story from the
Nibelungenlied, a medieval epic poem based in turn upon Teutonic legends
of pre-Christian antiquity. This present adaption—attempting to simplify
for children the Ring cycle's complex abundance of incident and character,
of psychological nuance and philosophical overtone—concentrates upon
the third opera, *Siegfried*.